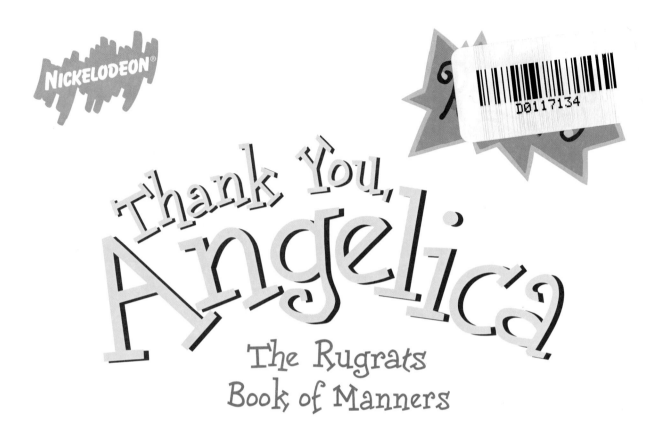

Thank You, Angelica

The Rugrats Book of Manners

by Cecile Schoberle
illustrated by Ed Resto

SCHOLASTIC INC.

New York Toronto London Auckland Sydney
Mexico City New Delhi Hong Kong

Based on the TV series *Rugrats*® created by Arlene Klasky, Gabor Csupo Inc. and Paul Germain as seen on Nickelodeon®

ISBN 0-439-09728-2

12 11 10 9 8 7 6 5 4 3 2 1   9/9 0 1 2 3 4/0

Printed in the U.S.A.   23

First Scholastic printing, November 1999

"Time for an afternoon snack," announced Didi Pickles, Tommy's mom. Tommy and his friend Chuckie were playing in the den.

"Oh, boy!" said Tommy. "Maybe it's Yummy Fruitso juice."

Didi brought in a tray with cups of fruit juice. "Angelica, would you please bring those cookies from the kitchen table?" she asked. Angelica, Tommy's cousin, carried in a big plate of fresh oatmeal cookies. "Of course, Aunt Didi," she replied in her sweetest voice.

Didi said, "Thank you, Angelica," and went back to the kitchen to bake some more cookies.

"I get to carry the plate of cookies because *I'm* grown up," said Angelica. "I know lots more than you babies do."

Chuckie looked over at the TV. On it, a queen in a fancy crown was smiling at people. "Why are those people bending their heads down?" asked Chuckie. "Did they lose something?"

"No! They have good manners," said Angelica.

Tommy asked, "What's 'manders'?"

"It's 'manners'!" yelled Angelica. "It means being extra nice."

"Hey, everyone, look how people are throwing flowers at the queen's car. I wonder if she'll throw back some of those colored rocks," said Chuckie.

"Of course not! She's not going to *share* her jewels," said Angelica.

"Mommy tells us to share our toys," said Tommy. "Is that good manders?"

"Manners!" yelled Angelica.

"Angelica," asked Chuckie, "does the queen have bad manners?"

Angelica shook her head. "You babies are driving me crazy!"

"Uh-oh, Angelica is mad," said Phil.

"Come on, Chuckie," said Tommy. "Let's share something. You can play with my ball. Can I play with your truck?"

"Vroom, vroom!" said Chuckie. He loaded up his dump truck with oatmeal cookies, and sent it rolling across the table. Faster and faster it raced toward Tommy.

"Uh-oh," said Chuckie. The dump truck screeched.

Wham! A big cookie flew out the back. It knocked the hat off Angelica's doll.

"Cynthia!" Angelica screamed.

Kersplash! The dump truck smacked into the cups, splashing juice all over the place. Spike wagged his tail and licked Angelica's juicy face. Tommy and Chuckie rolled on the floor and laughed.

"You babies have terrible, awful manners!" yelled Angelica.

"Gee, Angelica," said Tommy. "Could you get us good manders?"
Angelica frowned. She brushed oatmeal cookie crumbs out of
Cynthia's hair. "Well, maybe . . . I will show you how to play 'good
manners,'" she said. "But I must be . . . queen! And you babies will
serve me." She put on her Burger Doodle crown.

"Yay!" cheered Tommy. "We're gonna get good manders."

Angelica sat Cynthia in a tall chair. "Queen Angelica and Princess Cynthia would like another cookie, please," she said.

"Peas? But we don't have any peas!" said Chuckie.

"PLEASE!" yelled Angelica. "That word is the first good manner. And don't use that dumb dump truck."

Chuckie carefully gave Angelica a cookie. "Should I say something, Angelica?"

"Not yet! Wait your turn. You do what I say." She took a big bite out of the cookie. "Queen Angelica will now show you the second good manner. Your gracious queen says, 'Thank you.'"

Spike snuck up behind Angelica. He snatched her cookie and ran. "Stop it!" she yelled. "It's bad manners to play with food. Especially mine!"

Tommy leaped up. "I serve the queen. I will save her from the cookie-eating monster!" He started chasing Spike.

"No! No!" said Angelica. "It's *bad* manners to run around the table. Or to talk with your mouth full!"

"I'll get him, Tommy," said Chuckie. He leaned out of his chair and grabbed at Spike.

"Don't! Sit still! Sit up straight in your chair! I am a queen!" screamed Angelica.

Spike thought this was a fun game. He ran to Angelica and woofed in her face.

"Ooo, yuck!" squealed Angelica. "Cover your mouth when you cough."

Tommy and Chuckie lunged for Spike. "Look out!" Angelica yelled and jumped back.

Her beautiful Burger Doodle crown flipped off her head. "I'll get it, Your Majesty," called Tommy. He jumped up as high as he could.

"Awesome!" said Phil and Lil together.

"Let me, Your Highness," called Chuckie.

"Woof!" barked Spike.

"Be good! Act nice! Do what I say!" yelled Queen Angelica.

"Whoa!" yelled Tommy and Chuckie as they came down. Zoop!
The crown settled down right on . . . Spike's head!

Tommy and Chuckie laughed loudly. "Let's call him King Spike," said Tommy.

"You babies have terrible, awful, bad, bad manners!" scolded Angelica. "You spilled juice all over. And smushed the cookies. And knocked off Cynthia's hat. And now . . . you took my Burger Doodle crown!"

"Gee, Angelica. We didn't mean to. Did we, Tommy?" said Chuckie.

Didi walked into the room. "What a mess!" she said.

Angelica pointed her finger at the babies.

Tommy chuckled and
waved his hands.
Didi giggled. "Are you saying you're
sorry, Tommy?"
Chuckie did the same thing. "Isn't that nice?
Chuckie is sorry too," said Didi.

"Yeah, well, I'm more sorrier!" said Angelica.

Didi gave them all a big hug. "Such good kids! Such good manners!" she said.

Then Didi turned and saw Spike. "Mmm . . . that's funny," said Didi. "How did that crown get on Spike's head?"